Twas the Night Before Christ

Trina Bradford Phillips

Illustrated by: Alex Konoplev

AuthorHouse™
1663 Liberty Drive
Bloomington, IN 47403
www.authorhouse.com
Phone: 1-800-839-8640

First published by AuthorHouse 11/20/2012

ISBN: 978-1-4678-7167-9 (sc)
*   978-1-4772-9415-4 (e)*

Library of Congress Control Number: 2011961122

Printed in the United States of America

Any people depicted in stock imagery provided by Thinkstock are models,
and such images are being used for illustrative purposes only.
Certain stock imagery © Thinkstock.

This book is printed on acid-free paper.

authorHOUSE®

Twas the night before Christ,
And nobody would know,
Of the day or the hour.

That He'd come down to the earth,
To show his glory and power.

The sky was lit up,
With the Christmas night lights.

As the Angel sat high,
On top of the Christmas tree bright.

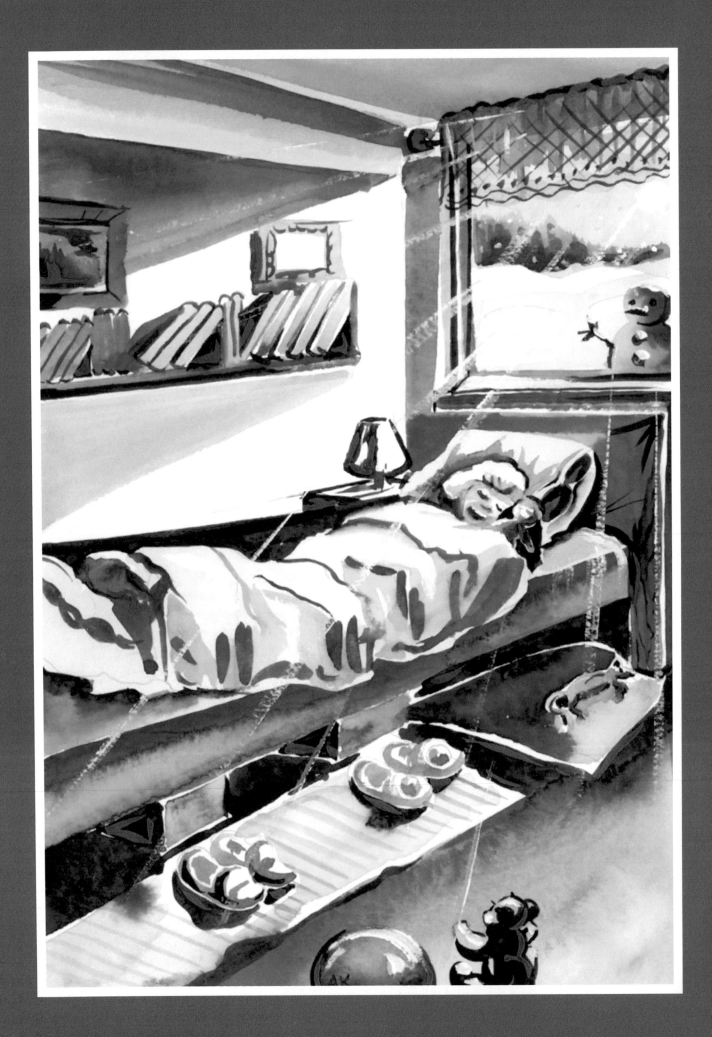

Twas the night before Christ,
As the family slept in the house.

Dot a creature made a sound
It was as quiet as a mouse.

The stockings were hung
By the fireplace neat,

And, there were chocolate
chip cookies for Santa, to eat.

Now, guess who was up top
Of the chimney chute,

Who shouted, "ho ho, uh oh,"
And off fell his boot.

With his big round belly,
He could not get free

Cause Santa Claus was
Trapped, up in the chimney.

So, he pushed and he pushed
Until he fell to the ground,

And he shook and shook,
When he heard the trumpet sound.

Santa Claus looked so silly,
Laying there with one boot

All covered with white ashes
From the chiminey chute.

Santa's nose began to twitch,
When he felt a great big sneeze.

So he reached for his nose
And he gave it a squeeze.

He let go of his nose,
With a sigh of relief,

And a great big, Aachooo,
Came and knocked down the tree.

Mom and Dad jumped out of bed,
And threw back the sheets,

They ran to the living room
To see what the noise could be.

Then the children awoke,
Cause it gave them a fright.

That's when they saw Santa
All covered in white.

With His cheeks bright and rosy
Like a rose petal bed,

And his nose round and shiny
Like the bump on his head.

When he came to himself
With a twist in his head.

Then there stood the Savior
Who had risen from the dead.

Santa Claus rubbed his eyes
And he scratched his grey head.

With his eyes fixed on Jesus,
This is what Santa, said.

Thank you Jesus, for being
The greatest gift in the world

Who came to save every
Man, woman, boy and girl.

So many children count on me,
This time of the year.

To bring the Christmas Spirit
And the Holiday Cheer.

I'm sent hundreds of letters
With the faith to believe.

Some of them ask, "Dear Santa,
why did Daddy leave?"

I knew that you'd take care
Of those specially marked letters,

Like the ones that say,
"Dear Santa, make Grandma feel better".

Only one day a year,
I bring joy and good cheer,

But your joy is forever
And your love brings no fear.

This is what Santa asked,
as he bowed down his knee.

Jesus, tell me, is there a place,
in your book of life for me?

Jesus said, I have checked it once
And I have checked it twice

Since all have done wrong,
In my father's sight.

Yes, I know of your faith
Your service and works,

And you remembered that
The last will be greater than the first.

He put his hand on Santa's shoulder,
As he spoke of God's love.

His love, is higher
Than the Heavens above.

It is deeper than the ocean
And wider than the sea.

Your sins are forgiven
And you have been set free

Tears of joy, wallowed up in
Santa's blue eye's.

Jesus grabbed Santa's hand
And looked up to the skies.

Jesus said, "I am pleased with
My love, you have shown,"

Now let's go to my Father
Who sits on the throne.

Then the angels of heaven
On white horses came,

And, Santa shouted out to the
reindeers by name,

It was Santa's prize reindeer,
Who lit up the way.

With his nose bright and shiny
To Heaven's pearly gates.

About the Author

Trina is a stay at home Mother and Entrepreneur. She has 3 children ages, 23, 18 and 13. Recently she became a grandmother of a beautiful baby girl named Maya. Trina's inspiration to write children's books came by reading to her children, and her love for sharing the gospel and serving in the Children's Ministry at her church.

CPSIA information can be obtained
at www.ICGtesting.com
Printed in the USA
LVIC06n0734231013
358140LV00001B/1